With love to Simon,
the Stringston shark

First U.S. Edition 2002
Published by Bloomsbury, New York and London
Distributed to the trade by St. Martin's Press

Library of Congress Cataloging-in-Publication Data
Newton, Jill, 1964-. Bored! Bored! Bored! / Jill Newton.–1st U.S. ed. p.cm.
Summary: With the neighborhood busy with gardening, Claude the shark is bored
until he finds a way to make his own contribution.
ISBN 1-58234-760-3
[1. Sharks–Fiction. 2. Fishes–Fiction. 3. Boredom–Fiction. 4. Individuality–Fiction.
5. Cookery–Fiction.] I. Title. PZ7.N48674 Bo 2002 [E]–dc21
LC 2001043985

Type set in Veronan
Printed in Hong Kong
1 3 5 7 9 10 8 6 4 2
First Impression

Bloomsbury USA Children's Books
175 Fifth Avenue
New York, New York, 10010

Bored! Bored! Bored!

Jill Newton

BLOOMSBURY
CHILDREN'S
BOOKS

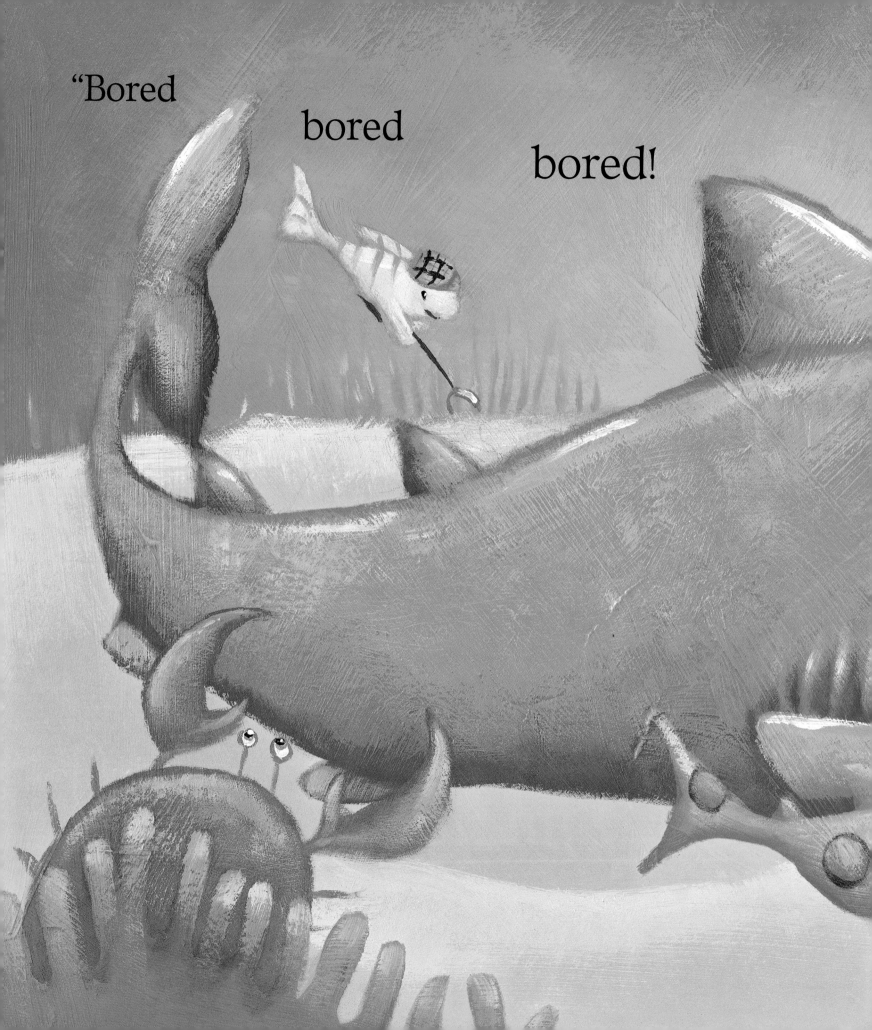

I'm SO bored!" wailed Claude the shark.

"How can you possibly be bored when there's always so much gardening to be done?" called the fish.
Claude yawned.

"Come and help us rake!" sang the seahorses.

Claude swam over to rake,

but soon he lost interest.

"Come and help us prune!" clacked the crabs.

Claude swam over to prune,

but he didn't really enjoy it.

"Come and help us plant!" waved the octopuses.

Claude swam over to plant,

but planting didn't seem to be his thing.

"Come and water the flowers!" fluttered the angel fish.

"No!" snapped Claude.
"I'm bored and I'm going home."

The sea creatures gardened until the sun started to go down, then they all admired the results.

The garden looked stunning.

The next evening the fish held a huge party for all those who worked so hard to keep the garden beautiful.

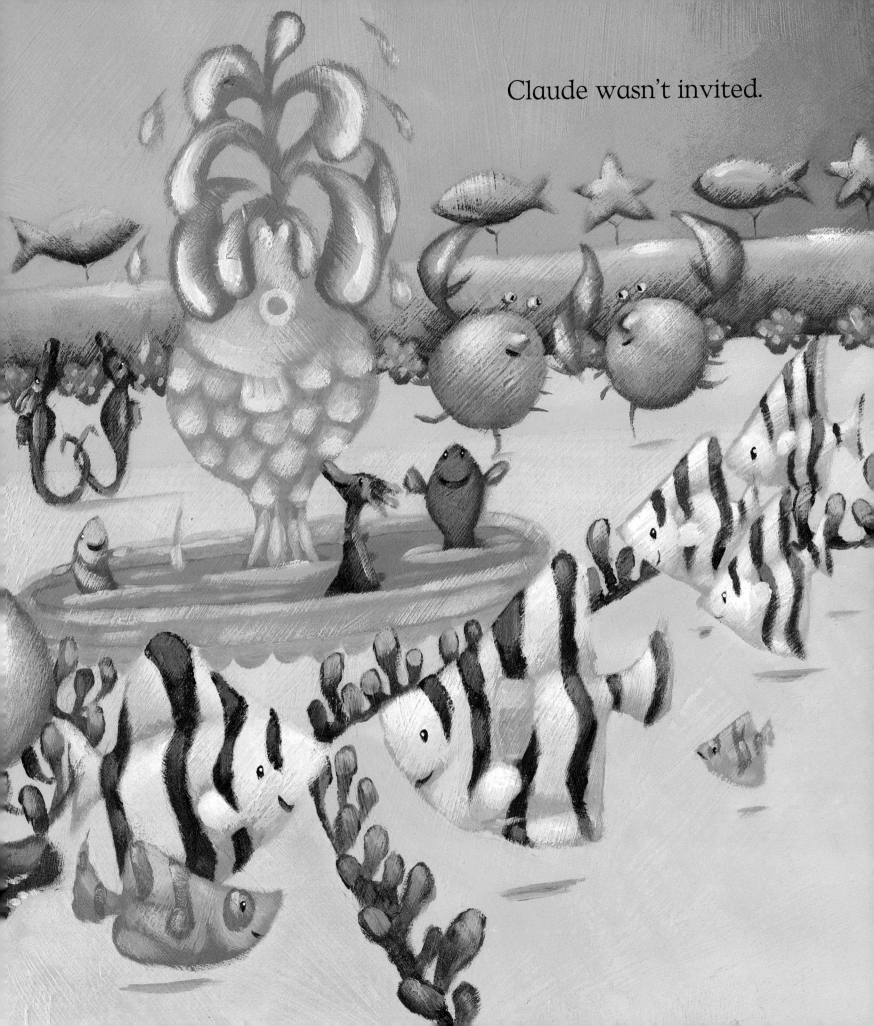

Claude wasn't invited.

Now Claude was

REALLY

bored.

He heard the singing and laughing
and music and felt sad and lonely.

Then he had a GREAT idea.

Claude went into his kitchen and started busily

mixing and **stirring** and

rolling and   **whisking** and

waited . . .

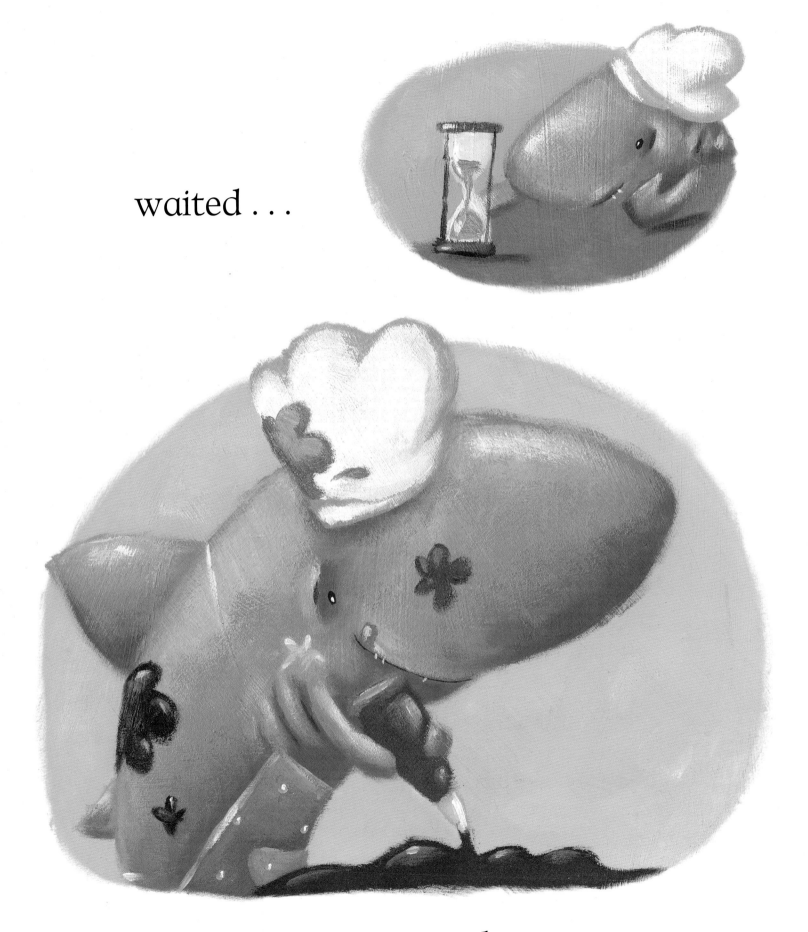

. . . and then iced.

When it was finished, Claude swam
to the party with what he had made.

"You made this?" sang the fish.
"But it's the most magnificent cake. It must have taken ages!"
"It was no trouble," said Claude. "I enjoyed doing it."

Claude joined in the celebrations . . .

. . . singing

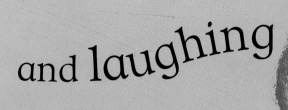

and laughing

and dancing.

The next day when the sea creatures went about their gardening chores, Claude was around to help.

Not **raking**

or **pruning**

or **planting**

or **watering** . . .

. . . but making snacks.